Ruby Rogers
is a Waste of Space

Ruby Rogers
is a
Waste of Space

Sue Limb

Illustrations by Bernice Lum

BLOOMSBURY

4160900

First published in Great Britain in 2006 by Bloomsbury Publishing Plc
36 Soho Square, London, WID 3QY

Text copyright © Sue Limb 2006
Illustrations copyright © Bernice Lum 2006
The moral rights of the author and illustrator have been asserted

All rights reserved
No part of this publication may be reproduced or
transmitted by any means, electronic, mechanical, photocopying
or otherwise, without the prior permission of the publisher

A CIP catalogue record of this book is available from the British Library

ISBN 0 7475 8321 8
9780747583219

All papers used by Bloomsbury Publishing are natural, recyclable
products made from wood grown in well-managed forests.
The manufacturing processes conform to the environmental
regulations of the country of origin.

Printed in Great Britain by Clays Ltd, St Ives Plc

1 3 5 7 9 10 8 6 4 2

www.bloomsbury.com
www.suelimbbooks.co.uk

CHAPTER 1

You idiot! You blinking idiot!

MY NAME'S RUBY ROGERS and I'm going to be a gangster when I grow up. Sort of like a modern Robin Hood, only female. I'm going to live in the treetops with my gang. I haven't thought of our name yet, but it'll be scary. We'll have swinging rope bridges and Tarzan-type vines up in the forest canopy. And whenever any horrible people come, we'll drop disgusting stuff on their heads.

We'll drop babies' dirty nappies and carrier bags full of sick. We'll pelt them with bombs made from bogeys. Then, when they're totally grossed out, covered with gunk and frozen with fear, we'll slide down the trees and steal their valuables. They'll run off screaming and we'll give all the money to a charity that helps kids.

Hmmm. Nice thought! And it was all going to begin today. I had a secret plan. OK, I may not be grown up yet, but inside my head I'm a gangster already.

It was the first day of the summer hols. The perfect moment to reveal my secret plan to my unsuspecting family. I had to tell them because I needed their help. Who would be the lucky person to hear it first? It would be awful if my big announcement was spoiled by somebody being In A Strop.

My brother Joe? Hmm. Not sure. Usually Joe is a bad-tempered, snarling, wild beast. But he'd been on holiday for ages already. The sixth form escape from school the moment their exams are over. He'd been out all day with his mates, doing something cool.

I knocked on Joe's bedroom door. There was a weird, sinister silence. No reply. I knocked again. 'You dirdy rat!' I drawled, trying to sound gangsterish. Still no answer. Maybe he was fiddling about with one of his dreary old projects.

Joe's into art. He makes little sculpture thingies out of wood. They're really models for great big enormous things, as big as a room. Or even bigger. His ambition is to make a huge Christmas pud by covering the dome of St Paul's Cathedral with yellow custard-type stuff and a gigantic sprig of holly. It's called 'installation art' apparently.

'Joe!' I called. 'Can I borrow a pencil?'

I couldn't just say, 'How was your day?' He'd smell a rat.

'Don't go in my room!' His voice came thundering out from the bathroom. 'Use your own stupid pencils!' I was annoyed. My pencils aren't stupid.

Joe didn't deserve to hear my secret. He had insulted my pencils. Besides, he would probably be in the bathroom for hours. He reads comic books in there.

'OK, OK, relax, why dontcha?!' I called gangster-ishly, and slouched off in search of Dad.

I thought Dad might be in the garden. You never quite know with Dad. Sometimes he sits on his bed, playing his guitar and trying to compose songs. The lyrics are usually something to do with city streets. *'A stranger stalks . . . the city streets . . . his name is George, no Fred, no Clive . . .'*

But Dad doesn't actually *like* being in city streets very much. We went to London for the day once, just him, Joe and me. Big mistake – Mum's the only one capable of organising a day out. Dad had a panic attack in the waxworks.

'I've got to get out!' he gasped, racing for the exit. Dingbat! Can you imagine anything more embarrassing?

Many people have dads who are the strong, silent type. My dad's the panicking, noisy type. He

only really relaxes in the garden. And he grows peas, which I like to eat raw, straight from the pod.

I found Dad in the garden shed. He was standing with his back to me, nailing something to the wall.

'SURPRISE, SURPRISE!' I shouted.

Dad jumped, hit his thumb instead of the nail, and let out a yowl of pain.

'You idiot!' he yelled, hopping about and cradling his hand. Dad's not very brave when it comes to injuries. 'You blinking idiot, Ruby! Never do that again!'

'Sorry, Dad!' I backed off, quick. I could see it wasn't the moment. Dad can lose it just like that. Even on an ordinary day he's only moments away from a full-blown panic. And he does hate hitting himself with a hammer. He's such a wuss. I decided to run indoors and talk to Mum. She was my only hope now.

CHAPTER 2
Frankly, this evening sucks

IF MUM'S IN A GOOD mood, somehow the whole house is. Although she's quite small, she bosses everyone about. She's a bit plump and she's got wild, curly, reddish-gold hair and a Welsh accent. She can be a bit strict about things being clean and tidy, but it's because she's a midwife. She spends all day delivering babies. It's a family joke: 'Did you have any nice babies today?' 'Oh no, love. I only had a rather nasty one that looked like a turnip.'

Thank goodness I'm not one of her patients. I'm

not going to have babies anyway. I'm going to have pets instead. Monkeys, mainly. They'll live with me in the forest canopy.

I found Mum asleep on the sofa. She often has catnaps after work. Waking her up is strictly against the rules. If you wake her, she's grouchy as anything. If you let her wake up naturally, in her own time, she's only *slightly* grouchy.

I watched her for a little while. She was lying on her back with her mouth half-open, frowning. Mum often talks in her sleep.

'Where's the nearest toilet?' she muttered, all of a sudden. *'That one's full of snakes!'* Same old dream! I sighed.

Suddenly I remembered that I hadn't tidied my room. I'm supposed to tidy it every day, but somehow I always forget.

I went upstairs. Not to tidy my room – obviously. I'd never do it without being nagged. I felt a bit low really. Not a single member of my family had been ready to share in my fabulous secret plan.

At times like this I like to hide in a den. The airing cupboard is a favourite location. I'm still small enough to curl up in the middle section, where the sheets and stuff are kept. I climbed up, pulled the door almost shut and closed my eyes in the darkness.

I thought about my secret plan. It was so exciting! If only I could tell somebody! I heard Joe come out of the bathroom and go back into his room. Right away he put on some loud, shouty music. I don't understand teenage boys. Thank goodness I'm not one. Besides, if I had been a boy, apparently I'd have been called Tristram after my uncle. He runs a bookshop in Bath and knits his

own ponchos. Not really a gangsterish role model.

Suddenly someone walked past the airing cupboard and pushed the door shut with a click. Immediately I panicked. Although I have inherited Mum's love of curling up somewhere cosy, I've also inherited Dad's fear of being shut in. The airing cupboard only opens from the outside! Ohmigawd! I was in danger of being aired to death!

'Heeeeeelp!' I yelled. Moments later, Mum flung the airing cupboard door open. Her face was still a bit crumply from her recent sleep.

'Oh, Ruby, get out of there!' she said grumpily. 'You'll crumple all my sheets! I spent hours ironing them!'

I scrambled out. I was tempted to growl, 'Iron yuh face, why dontcha, lady?' but it didn't seem like the right moment somehow.

'Supper is in ten minutes sharp!' said Mum. 'Tidy your room! I'm going to inspect it and if it's not tidy you won't get any supper!'

I didn't worry. I knew she would never knowingly starve a child. Mum does sometimes shout or snap, but she's not really strict underneath.

I went into my room, shut the door and lay down on my bed. My two monkeys, Stinker and

Funky, were lying on the pillow. Stinker is fat and bald and the boss. Funky is thin, woolly and very bendy.

'Stinker, Funky,' I told them sadly, 'it may be the first day of the hols, but frankly, this evening sucks.'

It wasn't the ideal moment to reveal my fabulous secret plan to my family. But I just *had* to tell somebody tonight. I needed grown-up help. My plan was that big. It was *immense*.

CHAPTER 3

I knew I was going to cry

SUPPER WAS PIZZA and salad. I ate some salad because I knew Mum was watching me. And there's nothing like eating healthy stuff to make your mum happy.

'That's right, petal!' she said. 'Lovely salad, isn't it?' She'd forgotten to inspect my room, of course. I could tidy it later anyway. I couldn't concentrate on anything else until I'd revealed my secret plan.

OK, Mum was in a better mood now, but Dad hadn't smiled at me since The Incident in the shed. Joe was glaring at his plate as usual, wolfing down his pizza like – well, like a wolf, I suppose.

Any minute now I would reveal my amazing secret. But I thought I'd better soften them up a bit first.

'I've decided to keep my room tidy for the whole holidays,' I said with a sneaky goody-goody sort of smile. Mum looked amazed.

'I'll believe it when I see it, petal!' she said, shaking her head. Although I quite like it when she calls me 'petal', she's going to have to stop all that nonsense when I'm a gangster.

'No, it's true,' I went on. 'I'm going to tidy my room every day after supper, round about eight o'clock.' Mum still looked pleased, but it was as if she'd already started to think about something else.

'Well done, then,' she said. 'Good girl. That's the spirit. Pass the salad dressing, please, Joe.'

'Did you have any nice babies today?' I said. The family joke.

'Oh yes,' she said. 'I had a lovely one with ginger hair all down his back.'

'Hmmm – sounds like a werewolf,' muttered Joe.

'The water heater's set too high,' said Mum to Dad. 'Can you adjust it? I nearly burnt my hands earlier.'

Dad looked startled. You could see he was beginning to panic.

'Couldn't we get a man in to do it?' he said. 'A proper man, I mean. With spanners and things. I think I need a spanner to do that. Where have my spanners gone, in fact? I haven't seen one for months.'

Joe finished his pizza with a greedy grunt, and drained his glass of juice.

'What's for pudding?' he asked.

'Yogurt or fruit,' said Mum defiantly. Joe groaned and dropped his head in his hands.

God, my family were so DULL! I had to reveal my magnificent idea to them now, to brighten up their tedious little lives.

'You know it's my birthday in a fortnight,' I said loudly, in a silence. They all looked at me kind of anxiously. Even Joe.

It was the moment of truth. It was so quiet, you could hear traffic going up and down the main road, miles away. My knees felt weak, even though I was sitting down.

'Well, come on, Ruby!' snapped Mum. 'We haven't got all night. What is it?'

'I want a tree house!' I said.

'A tree house, sweetheart?' said Mum. Her eyes went big and strange, and puzzled.

'In case you hadn't noticed,' said Joe, 'we haven't even got a tree.' He gave a mocking smile.

'It doesn't have to be in our garden,' I said. 'I realise that, obviously. I'm not a complete moron. It could be in any old tree in the countryside somewhere. Or in the park.'

'But if you had a tree house in the park,' said Mum, 'it wouldn't be just yours, would it, love?

Anybody could use it. Big rough boys could use it. They might not let you go anywhere near it.'

'Big rough boys would trash it,' said Joe.

'It wouldn't be allowed in the park anyway,' said Dad. 'Health and Safety regulations. You might fall out and hurt yourself.'

'Local Child Falls from Tree and Starts New Life as a Pizza,' said Joe. He often talks in newspaper headlines.

Dad went pale at the thought of my tragic fall and fiddled nervously with the pepper mill. I knew he was secretly trying to think of a song to be performed at my funeral. '*Oh, my beloved child, dear Ruby . . . She never lived long enough to roam the city streets . . .*'

Sadly, nothing rhymes with Ruby except Scooby. Or booby. Hardly a dignified funeral-type song.

'I could have a tree house out in the countryside, then,' I said. 'Or at Auntie Megan's house.'

Auntie Megan lives in North Wales, in a place with a weird long name that sounds like somebody sneezing. Something like *Lllantishoo!* It's lovely up there. She's got loads of trees in her garden. I climb them every time we go, in the summer hols.

'But we only go to Megan's for a week or so every year,' said Mum. 'And anyway, we couldn't just ask Megan if we could build a tree house in her garden. It would be rude, petal.'

'And anyway,' said Dad, 'if you're expecting me to build you a tree house, forget it. You know carpentry's not my strong point. I'm still reeling from my last injury.' He sucked his thumb.

'And Dad can't stand heights, remember,' said Mum.

'I can't even stand the thought of other people standing heights,' said Dad.

'So,' said Joe with a kind of sadistic grin. 'Looks like your tree house idea is a non-starter, huh?'

I knew I was going to cry. I jumped down from my chair, ran out and slammed the door. I raced upstairs to my bedroom, slammed that door too, grabbed my monkeys and hid under the bed. Then I burst into tears.

CHAPTER 4
Temper, temper!

WHEN I'D FINISHED CRYING, and I was just doing that sort of shuddering you get afterwards, I heard the TV being switched on downstairs. I knew I was going to get into trouble for jumping down from the table and slamming the doors. But not right now, it seemed. Nobody came.

Sometimes when Joe goes off in a strop and slams the doors, Mum just says, 'Leave him! Give him time to cool off.' She'd probably said the same thing about me.

Leabharlann
JH609 00
Contae na Midhe

I stayed under the bed. It's one of my best dens, although there's always a bit of a mess down there. In fact, right now, there were a few stale crisps in my hair. I could smell them – salt and vinegar. I grabbed my monkeys.

'OK,' said Stinker to Funky, in a gangsterish sort of voice. 'These cellars are right under da Houses of Parliament. We gotta seventeen boxes of high explosives. Gimme da matches.'

'Oh heck!' said Funky. 'I forgot the matches!' And he tried to make up for it by kissing his own ankles.

Suddenly there was a rough knock on my bedroom door. It was Joe's knock. It goes *Knock-knock! Knockety-knockety-knockety KNOCK!* I ignored it. Stupid boy! I lay still, under the bed, hoping he hadn't heard my monkeys talking.

Joe opened my door. There's no privacy in this house. I'd ask Dad to put a bolt on the door if he wasn't so useless at carpentry. I stared at Joe's feet, which were encased in rancid old trainers. No wonder he hasn't got a girlfriend.

'Great news,' said Joe. He knew I was under the bed. 'I've been looking at tree houses on the inter-net for you. They start at four thousand pounds and go up to twenty thousand. Amazingly cheap, huh? Won't take you long to save up, will it? Then all you have to do is plant the tree. Or maybe grow it from a conker.' And with a cruel laugh, he was gone.

A boiling wave of pure rage washed through me from top to toe. It was bad enough that Mum and Dad had so utterly dashed my hopes of a tree house. It was tragic that I'd been crying under my bed for what seemed like days. And what did my darling brother do? Twist the knife.

I crawled out from under the bed and jumped up, seething. I flung Stinker and Funky on the bed. Monkeys couldn't help at a time like this. It was up to me. I had to turn myself into a lean mean killing machine.

Joe and I often have fights, and I have to admit that so far it's Joe 299, Ruby nil. But I still attack him occasionally when he's been even more vile than usual. And this was one of those moments.

I burst out of my room. Joe was on the landing, holding a comic. I hurled myself at him, but he ducked sideways, jumped into the bathroom and locked the door.

'Temper, temper!' he jeered from within. He can whip me up into a white-hot fury. Suddenly I realised it was a waste of time waiting for him to come out of the bathroom and then attacking him. He'd only hit me back twice as hard.

I longed to drop something disgusting on his head. But there's never a carrier bag of sick around when you need one.

Wait! His bedroom was right there, at my mercy. I rushed in. His little art installation model thingies were everywhere. One was a model of a boat, designed to look like a bird. He'd spent ages on it. It had an eagle's head on the front, and along the side, instead of rows of oars, it had sort of wings.

'Stupid Schoolgirl Gets Stuck in Tree House!' Joe's voice called again, in a newspaper headline voice, from the safety of the bathroom – mocking, taunting. 'Fire Brigade Called. "I'll Never Leave Planet Earth Again," Sobbed the Tearful Tot.'

A wave of heat exploded in my tummy. I wanted to kill Joe. But he wasn't available. I brought my fist down on the bird boat and it splintered into pieces.

Instantly I felt sick. I felt sorry. The bird's neck had snapped and its head had fallen off. No matter how horrible Joe was, the little model itself looked sad and wrecked. It wasn't to blame.

I backed off quickly and rushed back to my own room and hid in the wardrobe, my heart thudding.

How was I ever going to be a gangster? This was my first crime (not counting the sweets I stole from Harry Mills' lunchbox), and I felt totally limp and horror-struck with guilt. I was going to have to toughen up, no question. Here I was, in a terrible state, and I'd only attacked a piece of wood.

Eventually I heard Joe come out of the bathroom and go into his room. There was a kind of pause when he must have seen what I'd done. I cringed in horror and ate a mouthful of my own winter coat. I knew he'd find me in the wardrobe in about three seconds flat.

His bedroom door burst open and I heard him storm out. My bedroom door burst open and I heard him storm in. I cringed so hard, my entire body shrank to the size of a two-year-old. Even Joe wouldn't lay a finger on a toddler, surely. But Joe didn't open the wardrobe door.

I heard a thump and a thud and a sort of scuffling noise, and after a moment he went out again and slammed my door. I waited in dreadful suspense. What had he done? Was he coming back for a second attack? Would he hit me this time?

I heard loud nasty music start up in his room. Phew! It seemed his raid was over. Gingerly, I ventured out to survey the damage. The first thing I saw was some wild red writing scrawled all over my dressing-table mirror. It read: *Ruby Rogers is a waste of space.*

Then I saw something ten times worse! Ohmigawd! Stinker's head had been pulled right off! It just lay there on the bed, staring at me, miles away from his poor bald fat old bod!

I was just about to burst into tears, when above

the sound of Joe's music, I heard Mum's voice down in the hall.

'Ruby! It's Yasmin on the phone!'

I raced downstairs. Yasmin's my best friend. Everything was kind of hectic today. Whatever next?

'Ruby! Listen!' said Yasmin. 'Guess who my sister brought home this afternoon? Holly Helvellyn!'

This was exciting! Holly Hellcat is a really weird girl who looks as if she might be our town's very own teenage witch.

'Tell me more!' I demanded. 'What's she like?'

'She didn't say much,' said Yasmin. 'But she's coming back tomorrow. She and Zerrin have got a holiday job just across the road. She's going to have lunch with us every day! Come over tomorrow and see for yourself!'

This was breathtaking. Holly Hellcat doing lunch at Yasmin's? I decided not to waste time crying about Stinker's head. I knew Mum would fix it back on, like she had when Joe had last ripped it off. I couldn't even think about monkeys at a time like this.

OK, so my main monkey was temporarily headless and my tree house plan was in ruins, but tomorrow I would go to Yasmin's and actually meet the amazing, the super cool, the fabulous Holly Helvellyn.

CHAPTER 5

She's so cooooool!

NEXT DAY I WAS over at Yasmin's like a shot. She lives in a town house near the city centre. On one side there's a car park. At the back they've got a huge garden with several really big trees. But we're not allowed to climb them. It's such a waste. One of Yasmin's uncles fell out of a tree once and broke his leg or something. And Yasmin's parents are quite strict about things like that.

Yasmin's more into dolls anyway. She's a bit clumsy, to be honest, and if she even *tried* to climb a tree, she'd probably end up with a branch up her jumper and a bird's nest on her head.

Yasmin's mum, Mrs Saffet, opened the door. She's beautiful, with black shiny shoulder-length hair. She always wears fabulous clothes. Today she was in a long grey dress and a billowing purple scarf. She is a big lady, though. If you were pretending to be her, you'd have to shove a whole pillow up your jumper.

'Ruby!' she cooed. She has a soft voice like a dove, and she says 'Ooooo!' quite a lot. 'Come in! Yasmin's just doing a liddle bit of tidying in her room. Go on up! Yasmin! Ruby's here!' (Yasmin's mum always says 'a liddle bit' of this and that. Perhaps it's because she's so big.)

I dived in, ducking under her enormous bosom, and ran upstairs. Yasmin's mum padded upstairs after me on her big velvety slippers. She has a study on the top floor where she works. She's a translator and she spends all day tapping away at her PC, surrounded by dictionaries.

Yasmin's bedroom door opened and Yasmin stood there grinning at me. She flung out her arms to hug me and banged her hand quite hard on the door.

'Ow! *Stinking Sickbags!*' she said, rubbing her

hand. Yasmin swears quite a lot. I knew she wasn't hurt too badly, though, because her worst swear word of all is, *'Blood and Guts and Dog Muck!'*

Yasmin's room is cheerful and white, and has wonderful sparkly cushions and turquoise curtains, and lovely mobiles hanging from the ceiling. My bedroom is basically a dump.

'Where's The Hellcat?' I whispered. Yasmin grinned.

'She and Zerrin have gone to work,' she said. 'They'll be back for lunch, though. She looks amazing! She's had another piercing – it's in her eyebrow. It's wicked!'

Yasmin and I had first noticed Holly Hellcat a few weeks ago in the park. A gang of us from our class were all playing cricket. It was a slightly insane version of cricket, with martial arts over-tones. And suddenly this Vision in Black strolled up and sat down under a tree to watch us.

She was quite tall, with dyed black hair arranged in a strange off-centre kind of rocket shape on top of her head, and carrying a camera. She had about a zillion bracelets and six earrings at least in each ear. Oh, and loads of silver rings. Her make-up was straight out of a horror movie.

Best of all I liked her lips: bright scarlet and shiny in the white mask of her face.

I was so distracted that for a moment I forgot to look out for the ball. It whizzed past my bat and the stumps flew everywhere.

'Out!' yelled the umpire. I didn't mind being out. Yasmin was out already. We spent the rest of the afternoon under a tree, watching the Vision in Black.

She was listening to her iPod. Sometimes she read a great big thick book with a picture of daggers on the front of it. Sometimes she

wandered around and took photographs. And sometimes she watched the cricket in a distant, slightly mocking way.

Later Yasmin's big sister Zerrin told us she was a mate of hers from school and her name was Holly Helvellyn. So she had to be The Hellcat, obviously.

She's so coooooool! I thought. And today I was actually going to have lunch with her!

'What's she like?' I asked.

'She's quite nice really,' said Yasmin. I felt a bit disappointed. 'She said, "Hi, how are you, Yasmin?" this morning and smiled at me. They'll be back at lunchtime. You can see for yourself.'

I couldn't wait for lunchtime. I helped Yasmin tidy her room. We even arranged all Yasmin's dolls in rows.

'Wanna play snakes and ladders?' asked Yasmin.

'Couldn't we play gangsters?' I asked. Yasmin frowned.

'Last time we played gangsters my mum was cross afterwards,' she said, 'because of the dolls being thrown about everywhere and the curtains being on the floor.'

'Look, it was a major crime scene,' I said. 'You can't use explosives without making a bit of a mess. OK, a few guys got hurt,' I started to drift into my gangster voice, 'but they was askin' for trouble. They was Big Al's henchmen.'

'I was the one who had to tidy up afterwards,' said Yasmin, pulling her stroppy face. She has a fiery temper and I try to avoid stirring her up.

We played Snakes and Ladders. After a while, she had a run of luck, went soaring up the biggest ladder and stopped frowning.

At last Yasmin's mum came down from her study. She stuck her head round the door and admired the room.

'Oooo, lovely!' she cooed. 'I've never seen Yasmin's room look so tidy! It's a total make-over! Thanks for helping, Ruby! There'll be a liddle bit of lunch in ten minutes.'

Then she went off downstairs and soon a yummy smell of soup came wafting up. We heard the front door slam and girls' voices downstairs. Zerrin and The Hellcat were back!

CHAPTER 6
Don't mess with him, babe!

W E BOUNDED DOWNSTAIRS and
ran into the kitchen.

'Hi, Ruby!' said Zerrin with a charming smile.
She is so nice. Amazingly pretty, with the family
hair: long, black and shiny. Her teeth stick out a
little bit, but she's got a brace at the moment so
that will be sorted. I love it when she shakes her
long hair about. My own hair is what Joe calls
'mousy rats' tails'.

The Hellcat looked at me and smiled. Her lips
were redder than ever.

'This is Holly,' said Zerrin graciously. Although she's very shy and gentle, she's always polite. 'Holly, this is Yasmin's friend Ruby.'

'Hi,' said Holly. Now she really looked *amazing*. She had the usual white face and red lips, and she was wearing a black lacy top that looked like a spider's web, and a purple velvet skirt.

'Hi,' I said, and – stupidly – blushed. It was like being introduced to the Queen or something. Up close, I could see that one of her rings was in the shape of a skull. Somehow I felt she ought to be living in a high tower overlooking a spooky lake, not sitting down at Yasmin's kitchen table and saying she was 'absolutely starving'.

The soup was great. Zerrin and Holly told us all about their new job packing airline meals.

'God, it's exciting!' said Holly sarcastically. 'I'm so tempted to snack on the little bits of cheese. And we get to wear these fabulous protective clothes – shower caps and white coats. *So* Ralph Lauren!'

I had somehow imagined Holly would be rather grand and silent, and not say much. But once she started chatting, she barely stopped for breath. Even Yasmin's mum couldn't compete.

'Your brother's going to art school, right?' she

said, suddenly looking straight at me. I almost choked on my soup.

'My brother?'

'Joe Rogers is your brother, isn't he?' asked Holly.

'Yes,' I admitted, my heart sinking. Joe is so awful I really didn't want people to know we're related.

'Holly worships Joe,' said Zerrin with a sly grin. 'What with him being in the sixth form and everything.'

'He's a legend,' said Holly. I was shocked. They had clearly never smelt his socks. 'How old is he?' Holly asked.

'Seventeen,' I said. It sounded so terribly, terribly old.

'When's his birthday?' asked Zerrin with a giggle.

'May 15th. Just a couple of months ago.' Holly and Zerrin exchanged a strange smile.

'I told you!' said Zerrin. 'He's a Taurus!'

'Wow!' Holly raised one of her perfect eyebrows. 'A bull! Watch out! Don't mess with him, babe! You could end up being gored!' They laughed again. In fact, they went into giggle over-drive.

'Steady on!' said Yasmin's mum, collecting the

soup dishes. 'Don't get hysterical. It could lead to indigestion. My uncle Sultan was laughing at a joke once, and he choked on an almond and nearly died.'

Everybody went a bit quiet at this story. I just hoped there weren't any almonds for pudding. It was nut-free, thank goodness: fruit salad.

'Now you girls can relax,' said Mrs Saffet, 'because you've had your five pieces of fruit and veg for the day.'

'I could eat fruit all day,' said Holly. 'I so adore it! I'm going to be a monkey when I grow up.'

Everybody laughed. I could hardly believe it. A monkey! We were obviously soulmates. She could certainly join my gang up in the canopy.

'Zerrin's going to be an astrologer when she leaves school,' said Yasmin.

'Oh, wow!' I said.

'Well, actually, of course, I'm going to do business studies,' said Zerrin in a sensible voice. 'But I'm going to do people's charts in my spare time.'

'Zerrin can tell what sign people are just by looking at them,' said Yasmin.

'Really?' I said. 'How amazing! What sign am I, then?'

Zerrin looked at me and frowned a bit, as if she

was trying to read my mind. Holly watched, fascinated.

'I can't always do it,' said Zerrin, tossing her long black hair back off her face. 'But I think you're either a Gemini or a Leo. Yes?'

'Wow!' I said, astonished. 'Yes! You did it! I'm a Leo. In fact, my birthday's in two weeks' time.'

'What are you going to get for your birthday?' asked Holly. 'Or is it a surprise?'

Suddenly I felt a little bit sad, even though Yasmin's kitchen was so bright and sunny and cheerful.

'I wanted a tree house,' I said. 'But my parents said no.'

'Harsh,' said Holly. 'Never mind. The same thing happened to me. I wanted a pet iguana, and my parents said no. But I'm going to get one anyway. That's why I've got this job. I'm saving up for an iguana.'

'Can we have an iguana, Mum?' asked Yasmin.

'NO!' said Yasmin's mum, laughing. 'You know the rules. No animals in the house. Not even a liddle tiny one.'

'Apart from Dad, of course,' said Zerrin. We all laughed. Dads are rather animal-like sometimes. I'm a bit afraid of Yasmin's dad, to be honest. It's his moustache. But he's also quite strict. Thank goodness he was out at work. He's rich. He sells fitted kitchens (which is one reason why Yasmin's kitchen is so beautiful). My dad is a bit of a wimp compared to Yasmin's dad, but I wouldn't swap them for anything.

I felt more cheerful as we finished lunch. Holly had inspired me. I wasn't going to give up my plan just yet. There had to be a way to make it come true. There just *had* to.

CHAPTER 7

I've had a brilliant idea!

AFTER LUNCH WE WENT out into Yasmin's back garden and made a den. There's a table out there where they have meals sometimes in hot weather. Yasmin's mum gave us some old curtains and we draped them over the table so they hung down the sides. We put a blanket on the floor. It was like a tent.

'You be the footballer going out to work,' said Yasmin. 'I'll be the wife – wait! I'll go and get some dolls. We'll have seventeen sons and twenty-three daughters.' She ran off. I stayed in the den. I didn't want to get into an argument over the size of our family. Soon she reappeared, carrying all our children in a box. I tried hard to look interested.

'OK,' said Yasmin. 'They're called David, Victoria, Britney, Beyoncé, Jude, Jason, Kylie, Vince, Harry . . . er . . .'

'OK, OK,' I said. 'I'm off to practice now. Apparently the manager's thinking of selling me to Chelsea so by the end of the week we could be celebrating!'

'Great,' said Yasmin. 'I'll book a table at the Ritz. I'm going to relax on the patio all day.'

'Fine,' I said. 'I'm off, then.' And I went off down the garden and pretended to kick a ball about. I could hear Yasmin in the den, talking to the dolls. She seemed to be telling them off. I feel sorry for her future children.

After a while I completely forgot I was supposed to be a footballer. I looked up into a tree. It was beautiful up there. I almost envied the birds. My tree house seemed a total impossibility.

But then I thought of Holly. She had her heart set on an iguana. She was earning money to buy one. She hadn't taken 'no' for an answer. She was lucky though. Teenagers get jobs all the time. It's so unfair. If only I could go to work in the factory with Zerrin and Holly, I might earn enough money to pay for a tree house. But I was too young.

I wanted to get rid of this sad mood, so I strolled over to the hedge and peeped through into the car park. There was nothing exciting to see: just rows of parked cars. Some of them looked dusty in the sunlight. There was one which was so dirty, somebody had written 'clean me' in the dust.

Suddenly I almost jumped out of my skin. That

was it! We could clean cars! There wasn't a law against small kids cleaning cars. I might make enough money to buy a tree house – or build one somewhere.

'Hey, David! When are you coming home?' Yasmin called. She was kneeling at the entrance to the tent. I ran back to her. She threw her arms around me and gave me a smacking kiss.

'Get off!' I yelled. 'I've had a brilliant idea!'

'Where are we going for dinner?' asked Yasmin. 'The Ritz? Or shall we nip over to Paris? Shall I ask Jeeves to get the plane out?'

'No, never mind that!' I said excitedly. 'Listen! We could wash cars for money!'

Yasmin looked puzzled.

'What for?' she asked.

'If I can make enough money during the school holidays, I might be able to get a tree house!' I said.

Yasmin looked a bit bored and cross. 'Look, Ruby, I'm really sorry that you can't have your tree house,' she said. 'But you haven't even got a tree. I mean, where do you start?'

'There are lots of trees out in the country,' I said.

'But trees out in the country still belong to somebody,' said Yasmin with a slight scowl. 'Farmers or whatever.'

'Well, I'll rent a tree from the farmer then. Have you got a bucket? Let's start now!'

And I ran straight indoors and upstairs to Yasmin's mum's study. Yasmin followed. We burst in, panting. Yasmin's mum was sitting at her computer.

Pleasecanwehaveabucketofwater?' I yelled. 'So we can washcarsformoney?'

'Steady on!' said Yasmin's mum, laughing. 'Now,

slow down a liddle bit, get your breath back and start again.'

Once she'd understood what we were asking, Yasmin's mum sort of sighed, smiled, and tried to look kind and sympathetic. I just knew she was going to say NO.

'The thing is,' said Yasmin's mum, 'we've got to be a liddle bit careful. Your safety is the most important thing. You'd be washing cars for strangers.'

'We could ask the neighbours first,' said Yasmin. 'We could wash their cars. We'd be safe with them.'

'Great idea!' I said. 'Let's start right away!'

But sadly, it was time to go home. I had to leave early because Yasmin had a dentist's appointment. Yasmin's mum dropped me off on the way. As I got out of the car, she said, 'Now, Ruby, make sure you parents know about this car-washing idea, OK?'

I nodded, but I wasn't looking forward to mentioning it. I had a feeling that Mum and Dad would think of all sorts of stupid objections.

CHAPTER 8

I don't like the sound of her

'**Y**OU'RE LATE!' SAID MUM when I got in. She was chopping up some onions and her eyes were streaming. I could tell by her face that she had had a horrid day.

'Sorry, Mum,' I said. 'Did you have any nice babies today?'

'We had a bit of a crisis,' said Mum. 'It was all right in the end, but I'm shattered. Go and tidy your room,' she snapped. 'It's a disgrace!'

I went upstairs. As usual I was depressed by my

room. I hate the wallpaper, which is really baby-ish. There are places where I scribbled on the walls when I was young. So embarrassing. And there's always a terrible mess. The floor was covered with toys and clothes. I scooped them all up into a couple of carrier bags and hid them in the wardrobe.

Mum had put Stinker's head back on last night, but now he was lying face down on the floor. Funky was lying with his face in Stinker's bottom. How awful for them. I know monkeys aren't quite as civilised as us, but they do have some standards.

I felt so guilty, I decided to organise a gangsters' banquet for them. I made a kind of shady veran-dah out of my sock drawer by turning it on its side. Just the sort of place gangsters might hang out on a hot evening. The socks had to be tipped out all over the floor, but never mind.

I sat Stinker and Funky down on the verandah and laid a picnic for them with a dolls' tea set. Halfway through the meal, though, Stinker collapsed.

'The lasagne!' he gasped. 'It was-a poisoned! Big Al wuz behind dis! Sack da caterers! And ring for da ambulance!'

Then suddenly Mum came bursting in and the whole room shook, and the drawer fell over, trapping the monkeys and ruining their poisoned banquet.

'I told you to tidy your room!' said Mum in a horrid snarly voice.

'I did!' I protested.

'Well, look at it!' said Mum, pointing at the socks and tea cups scattered everywhere, and the upturned drawer.

'I did tidy it up, honestly,' I said. 'This is just a new mess.'

Then Mum went bananas. In fact, I think I'd better draw a veil over the rest of that scene. I didn't mention my plan to wash cars. It wasn't the moment.

It was spaghetti bolognese for supper. Joe wolfed his down as usual. He didn't look at me. He'd been blanking me since I trashed his boat-bird installation art model thingy.

'A glamorous girl was asking after you today,' I said to Joe. He looked up, blushed, and scowled.

'What?' he said. 'Who?'

'Holly Helvellyn,' I said. 'Known as The Hellcat.'

'Never heard of her,' said Joe, and went back to his spaghetti.

'I don't like the sound of her,' said Mum. 'Holly what? She sounds like a bit of A One.'

'She's *sooo* nice,' I said. 'A bit gothic, that's all. You know who she is, Joe. The one with black hair and red lips and all those piercings.' Joe ignored me.

'Pass the sauce, please,' said Dad.

'I've made a blinking sauce, Brian!' snapped Mum. 'It's an insult to put extra sauce on it.'

'What's for pudding?' growled Joe.

'There isn't a pudding,' said Mum menacingly. Quite gangsterishly, in fact.

It was so *not* the moment to ask about the car washing. Dad and Joe finished their dinner as fast as possible.

'OK. How about a driving lesson, then?' Dad asked Joe. 'As I've mysteriously lost the will to live, let's go now.' Joe leapt up eagerly.

'Yeah,' he said. 'I want to practise those three-point turns.' Seconds later, they were gone. Mum sighed.

'Relax, Mum,' I went on. 'I'll load the dishwasher. You go and sit down.'

'Thanks, love,' said Mum, and patted me on the head. 'I've got to admit it, I'm tired out.' She got up stiffly and strolled off to the sitting room. I heard her switch on the TV.

When I'd finished loading the dishwasher and wiped down the table, I went into the sitting room. Mum was asleep on the sofa. She stirred in her sleep, smacked her lips and muttered something that sounded like, '*No thanks, I'll go in the next one.*'

'Mum?' I said.

'Hhhhrrrrrrph?' said Mum.

'Is it OK if Yasmin and I wash people's cars for money?'

'Mmmmmmnargh,' sighed Mum, and settled back into sleep.

I decided to take that as a YES.

CHAPTER 9
It's all your fault!

THE NEXT DAY my mum dropped me off again at Yasmin's house. Yasmin's mum was wearing a floaty dark green tunic with wide floppy trousers.

'My mum said it was OK for me to wash cars!' I said right away.

'Fine,' said Yasmin's mum. 'Yasmin's share is going to help the children in Africa.'

Uh-oh! If Yasmin was helping children in Africa, but I was collecting money for myself, it made me feel as if I was horrid and selfish. I was really

53

sorry for the children in Africa, but I *so* wanted my tree house.

'I've got to go and work upstairs for a liddle while,' said Yasmin's mum. 'Why don't you start with Mrs Fisher opposite?' Yasmin's mum gave us buckets of soapy water and rags and sponges, and we went out.

'We clean one car at most,' growled Yasmin as we went up the neighbours' path. 'And then we stop, right? I'm sick of it already.'

Mrs Fisher answered the door, holding a baby and with a toddler clinging to her legs. A great blast of stinky air hit us in the face. The baby's nappy definitely needed changing. I'm never having babies. Unless the government sends someone round to deal with the poo.

We explained what we were doing and Mrs Fisher looked doubtful.

'I'm a bit short of cash at the moment,' she said. 'I know our car is ever so dirty, but . . .'

'Never mind, then,' said Yasmin. 'It's fine. Don't worry.' And she backed away, looking relieved.

'Oh dear, no, Yasmin, I feel so mean,' said Mrs Fisher. 'I must help. Those poor African orphans! I hate to think how Jasper and Cleopatra would cope if anything happened to me.'

She disappeared and came back with fifty pence. *Fifty pence!* What an insult.

'Thanks very much!' said Yasmin, trying hard to smile. As soon as Mrs Fisher had gone back indoors, Yasmin lost her temper.

'Blood and Guts and Dog Muck!' she said. 'We've got to clean this whole car now for peanuts! I never wanted to wash cars anyway! It was your idea! And I can't even keep my share! This is the worst day of my life and it's all your fault!'

She did have a point. I just buttoned my lip and we set to work on Mrs Fisher's car, which hadn't been washed for about a year. We needed buckets and buckets of clean water from Yasmin's house and Yasmin's mum had to find some clean rags for us because the ones we started out with soon turned totally black.

It took ages, and Yasmin's mood got worse and worse. She hurt her elbow on the wing mirror and she tipped a bucket of water all over her shoes.

By the time we'd finished Yasmin was totally stressed out. But the car really gleamed. It looked a million times better than the old heap it had been an hour before.

'Let's tell her we've finished,' I said. 'Maybe she'll be so pleased, she'll give us a bit extra. If she does, you can have it all.' I thought this was really generous of me, but Yasmin didn't even say thanks.

When Mrs Fisher answered the door, it was obvious that the baby had just been sick on her shoulder. What is it with babies? Horrible stuff coming out of them all the time! You could almost do a bank robbery using a baby instead of a gun.

'OK, *gimme da money or I fire da baby! From both ends!*'

Mrs Fisher kind of glanced at the car. She couldn't really concentrate properly on anything with the baby screaming in her ear.

'Brilliant! Well done!' she said. 'You can come back and do it again next month. Good luck with it! I hope you get lots of takers!' Then she went back inside and shut the door in our faces.

'Oh well,' I said. 'We've still got twenty-five pence each. That's not bad.'

'It wouldn't even buy a packet of crisps,' said Yasmin grimly.

'So, where next?' I said, looking around. 'There's a dirty car over there.'

'Lunch next,' said Yasmin firmly. 'I am never going to clean a car again in my entire life.' My heart sank. It seemed as if the tree house fund was a complete failure.

CHAPTER 10
You look like a film star!

I DIDN'T MIND STOPPING really. To be honest, I was tired and hungry myself. As we went back to Yasmin's house, we met Zerrin and Holly coming back from work.

'We've been washing cars,' I said. 'We've earned fifty pence.'

'Wow! Good work!' said Holly. She made it sound like a triumph instead of a disaster.

Jacket potatoes were on the menu, with a lovely banana and coconut pudding. Yasmin's mum finished her lunch quickly and went back upstairs to finish off her work project.

'So, how's the charismatic Mr Rogers?' asked Holly, looking at me with twinkling eyes. I was puzzled. Why was she asking about my dad? And what did 'charismatic' mean?

'What's "charismatic"?' asked Yasmin.

'Oh, you know – attractive and glamorous and stuff,' said Holly. 'But kind of quiet and mysterious as well.'

'Joe's a bit of a legend in our year group,' said Zerrin.

Oh! It was *Joe* they were asking about, not Dad. Thank goodness we'd cleared that up. I could easily have said something really silly.

'I didn't see much of Joe yesterday,' I told her. 'He went out for a driving lesson right after supper, and when he came back he shut himself in his room. I expect he was busy with his sculpture thingies.'

'He's having driving lessons?' Holly's eyes lit up.

'I can see him collecting you in a sports car, Hol!' said Zerrin, laughing.

'Yeah!' said Holly, flashing her eyes. 'A coupe or whatever they're called. A primrose-yellow Porsche.'

'Joe's never going to have a car of his own,' I

said. 'We couldn't even afford a primrose-yellow primrose.'

'What driving school is your brother with?' asked Holly.

'Oh, he's not with a driving school at all,' I said. 'Dad's teaching him for nothing.'

'My God! Lucky guy!' said Holly.

'Who do you mean? Joe or his dad?' said Zerrin with a teasing look at Holly. The way Zerrin and Holly behaved, it was obvious that Holly's crush on my brother was worse than I'd thought. It must be like . . . some sort of *sickness*.

'My dad's refused point blank to go in the car with my bro Tom,' said Holly. 'Tom's already failed twice. We're high achievers, us Helvellyns.'

'My dad panics all the time about everything,' I said. 'It must be a nightmare being taught to drive by him. But Joe doesn't seem to mind.'

'I'd love to swap lives with you, Ruby!' said Holly with a witchy wink. 'Just for twenty-four hours. Just for a laugh.'

'Why?' I asked. Holly pulled a funny not-going-to-tell face.

'Can't you guess?' said Zerrin. 'It's because you live in the same house as the charismatic Joe!' She fluttered her eyelashes at Holly, and they both laughed.

'Tell you what, Ruby,' said Holly with a playful glint in her eye. 'You couldn't do me a small favour, could you? You couldn't steal a little something from Joe's room for me?'

'Steal something? Like what?' I asked.

'Like a pillowcase his head has rested on or something,' said Zerrin. 'I'm sure Holly would pay good money for a souvenir like that!' They both went off into fits of giggles.

I made plans to steal one of his pencils and sell it to the highest bidder. Hmmmm . . . Nice thought. Although I was a bit wary about going anywhere near my brother's room right now. He was still ignoring me since the horrible way I'd trashed his bird-boat.

Yasmin refused point-blank to do any more car-washing, so to keep her sweet I pretended to be a press photographer all afternoon, doing lots of fashion shoots with her. Then I pretended to be a TV interviewer asking her about her latest collection of swimwear and leisure outfits, even though fashion bores me so much I felt like screaming aloud. It was such a relief when it was time for *The Simpsons*.

Mrs Saffet couldn't give me a lift home because her car was having its MOT, so when Holly got back from work, she offered to see me to the bus stop. It was on her way anyway.

'So, what sort of day have you had?' she asked. 'How's the tree house fund?'

'Useless,' I said. 'I've only got twenty-five pence, and Yasmin won't wash cars any more so that's it really.'

'You don't have to wash cars,' said Holly. 'You could do loads of other stuff to make money. Run errands for people, do paintings on the pavement, or face paintings . . . walk dogs . . . babysitting?'

'I can't do babysitting,' I said. 'I'm not old enough. In the eyes of the law I'm still a stinking baby myself.' Holly roared with laughter.

'You're priceless, Ruby,' she said. 'How old are you anyway?'

'Twenty-eight,' I said. Holly laughed again. She's easily amused – one of the reasons I like her so much.

'Wow, look at that!' said Holly suddenly. We were passing a charity shop, and in the window was a black hat with a veil. 'We've got to go in!' Holly pulled me along with her.

While she tried on the hat, I looked around. Suddenly my heart gave a huge leap. There, grinning at me from a cardboard box, was the most marvellous monkey! He was wearing a baseball cap and carrying a tennis racket. His eyes were little black shiny beads. I picked him up and cuddled him. He smelt nice. How could anybody ever have parted with him?

'How's my hat?' said Holly.

'You look like a film star!' I said.

'What an adorable monkey!' said Holly.

'I collect monkeys,' I said. 'But I can't afford him.'

'I'll buy him for you!' said Holly. 'He's divine! We can call him Hewitt!'

I watched, amazed, as Holly the Hellcat, the coolest person in town, bought me a monkey!

'Thanks,' I said. 'Thanks so much! If there's anything I can ever do to make it up to you . . .'

'You're already going to do something,' said Holly as we walked out of the shop, arm in arm. She was wearing her film-star hat and I was clutching Hewitt. It was one of the most exciting moments of my life. 'You're going to do something amazing and brave for me, aren't you, Ruby?'

For a moment I wondered what she was talking about. She leant in close and whispered in my ear: 'You're going to nick something from Joe's room for me, remember? Just for a joke. I want it tomorrow morning at twelve thirty sharp when I get in for lunch at Zerrin's!' And she laughed as if it was the best joke ever.

But the whole idea filled me with a horrid sick feeling, as if something awful was bound to happen.

CHAPTER 11

What amazing stuff!

WHEN I GOT HOME, Mum was sitting at the kitchen table having a cup of tea. Joe was also there, reading a comic and drinking a cappuccino. Uncle Tristram gave us an Italian coffee maker last Christmas. Mum prefers tea, Dad nearly broke it and had a panic attack, but Joe uses it all the time.

There was a faint smell of curry. Great! I love curry. I'm going to go to India when I grow up and try all the different sorts.

'Have you made a curry, Mum?' I said, kissing her.

'No,' said Mum. 'The good news is, somebody else made it. It's a ready meal. All I have to do is make the cucumber raita.'

'Did you have any nice babies today?' I asked.

'I had twins today,' said Mum, pouring another cup of tea. 'They looked a bit froggy actually.'

'Woman Gives Birth to Toads,' said Joe in his newspaper headline voice. 'Father Says, "There may be half a million of them but we love them all equally."'

'Do you love us equally, Mum?' I asked.

'Of course she doesn't,' said Joe, getting up. 'I'm the glamorous firstborn, loser!' And he hit me over the head with his comic as he walked off. I was quite pleased really. It didn't hurt, and it seemed he'd forgiven me for trashing his model. But would he ever forgive me for what I was planning to do now? Steal something! Would I have the guts to do it?

'What's that monkey?' asked Mum. 'Is it one of Yasmin's?'

'No, Holly bought it for me in the charity shop on the way home,' I said.

Mum frowned. 'Who's Holly again?' she asked.

'She's a friend of Zerrin's. She's amazing. She wears black and she has this Gothic make-up and she's got a nose ring and a eyebrow ring,' I said.

Mum pulled a face. 'I remember. I don't like the sound of her,' she said.

'Oh, but she's lovely, Mum! She saw me to the bus stop because Mrs Saffet's car was having its MOT.'

Mum still looked rather stern and shook her head disapprovingly.

'I don't like it when young girls disfigure their lovely faces with all those horrible piercings,' she said. 'You'd better not even think about it when you're a teenager, Ruby.' And she got up and started chopping a cucumber. 'Go and tidy your room,' she went on. 'It's worse than ever today.'

I went upstairs feeling cross. Mum didn't like the sound of Holly just because of her Gothic style. That was so unfair! Holly was so amazing. And she wasn't rude or nasty or anything. She was always really polite to Yasmin's mum.

My room looked terrible. There was a mountain of dirty clothes, toys, crisp packets, comics and books. I found Stinker and Funky under the pillow and introduced them to Hewitt.

'Hi guys!' said Hewitt. 'I just blew in from Oxfam. How's tricks?'

'OK . . .' Stinker looked him up and down.

'What can you bring to da organisation?'

'I got a tennis racket,' said Hewitt. 'Plus I got charisma. What more do you want?'

'I could use a guy wid charisma,' said Stinker. 'Welcome to da firm.'

They shook paws. The deal was done. Hewitt was now officially a member of the gang.

The curry was great. Mum had forgotten all about Holly, and she was chatting away about when we were going to stay with Aunt Megan in Llantishoo.

'It's not till the last week of August,' she said. 'So there's plenty of time before then for you to get a job and earn a bit of money, Joe. Dad and I work our fingers to the bone, and we don't like to see you lying in bed till midday.'

'Don't look then,' said Joe.

'Don't be cheeky! I mean it, mind. You jolly well get out of bed and get yourself a job, or there'll be trouble.'

'Midwife Kills Son with Papadom,' said Joe. Mum looked exasperated.

'Tell him, Brian!' she said. Dad flinched slightly and looked awkward.

'Do as your mother says, is my advice, old bean,' he said. 'Or I'll never give you another driving lesson as long as I live.'

'How about one after supper, then?' said Joe.

'Done,' said Dad. 'Anything to avoid the dish-washer duties.'

'Wait! You've got to clear the table first,' said Mum. 'Ruby had to do it last time.'

'Well, what else is she good for?' said Joe.

He and Dad did load the dishwasher this time, though, and Mum went off to the sofa for a snooze.

I went upstairs and lurked in my room. My

heart was beating fast. All I had to do was take something from Joe's room while he was out having his driving lesson. This was the perfect moment. My life of crime was about to begin.

I tiptoed to Joe's room. I hadn't been in here since that awful day when I'd trashed one of his models. The first thing I saw was that very same model, held together with thread and pins. He had glued it together again and put it on the windowsill to dry. I felt a horrid pang of guilt.

But I had to forget about that. Right now I had to find something for Holly. The pillowcase was out of the question. Even if Joe didn't notice it straight away, Mum would go bananas when she found it was missing. On the floor were a pair of dirty socks. I picked one up and sniffed. Minging! Gross! A total stench! I dropped it and looked around. What wouldn't he miss?

The room was completely and utterly crammed with his model thingies. Boats and planes and kites and buildings all mixed up with animals and birds and fishes. There were boats that looked like frogs. Planes that looked like eagles. And even a tiger on wheels. I had to admit it was amazing stuff.

I knew that in his wardrobe Joe had even more

models stashed away – ones he'd made last year. I opened the wardrobe door. It creaked slightly. I paused and listened. Not a sound from downstairs. The models were stacked carefully, but there were so many, surely he wouldn't miss one. It would be the perfect thing to give Holly. Not too personal, like clothing. And she was arty too, so she'd probably like that kind of thing.

One small one caught my eye. It was a kind of duck, but a bit like a skeleton of a duck, so you could see inside it. Inside was a blue egg, but the egg was made of sort of glass stuff, and inside the egg you could see a weird eye looking out at you.

Somehow I felt this would be the perfect thing for Holly. I picked it up carefully and crept back to my own room. I knew there were some shoe boxes in the bottom of my wardrobe, with Lego in. I tipped out the Lego and the bird sculpture fitted in just perfectly. I put the lid back on and hid it under a couple of T-shirts in the bottom of my wardrobe.

I'd done it! But I had started to feel totally, totally terrifed.

CHAPTER 12
Why are you blushing?

I DECIDED TO GO downstairs and met Mum on the way up. Phew! That was close! If she'd been five minutes earlier she'd have caught me red-handed.

'Why are you looking so guilty?' she said, giving me a sharp look.

'Er – I haven't tidied my room yet,' I said. Mum pushed past me and flung open my bedroom door.

'Honestly, Ruby!' she said. 'Lego all over the floor! For goodness' sake, clear it up! You could tread on that and hurt your foot!'

I went back to my room and put all the Lego pieces in my underwear drawer, under my vests. I would sort everything out properly one day.

Next morning I felt nervous. I had one main task: to smuggle Joe's sculpture out of the house and get it over to Holly.

'Get a move on,' said Mum. 'If I'm going to drop you off at Yasmin's, we have to leave NOW.'

'Wait a min!' I raced upstairs and took the shoe box out of its hiding place. There was no sound from Joe's room. He sleeps till twelve some days. I rushed downstairs and jumped into the car.

'What's in that box?' asked Mum, starting the car. I felt myself blush.

'Only Lego,' I said.

'Why are you blushing?' asked Mum, driving off.

'Because I forgot to tidy my room again,' I said. It wasn't even a lie. I had tried on six different tops this morning and the five I hadn't chosen were flung about everywhere.

Mum sighed, but then she had to start concentrating on the traffic so I didn't have any more hassle till we got to Yasmin's.

Once Yasmin and I were alone in her room, I opened the box. Yasmin stared at the model.

'It's amazing!' she said. 'He's so clever! How did he do it?'

'I dunno,' I said. But I felt pleased. Although most of the time I feel like punching Joe quite hard in the mouth, I do like it when people praise him. Especially Yasmin. She can be kind of hard on people.

Yasmin wanted to spend the whole morning dressing up her dolls as a rock band. I went along with it. Secretly, though, I was longing for lunchtime when I could show Joe's model to Holly. Eventually the magic moment came. I put the shoe box on the table in front of her. She lifted the lid and stared inside. Then, very carefully, she lifted it out.

'Amaaaaaazing!' said Holly as she stared at the wooden duck-skeleton thing. 'It's just amazing! Joe's a genius! What is he *like*?'

'Yeah, well,' I said, shrugging. 'He's just always made models. He started off on kits, but about two years ago he started just making up his own.'

'He's so talented!' said Holly.

'What's that?' asked Yasmin's mum, bringing some falafel to the table.

'Ruby's brother made it!' said Zerrin. 'He's in the sixth form. He's a genius!'

Yasmin's mum peeped at the model from different directions. She held it up to the light.

'Oh, my goodness, Ruby,' she said. 'Your brother has a great imagination. But it's a liddle bit fragile. I'm surprised he let you bring it. What if you broke it?' She cringed and pulled her anxious face.

'I'm just borrowing it for a bit,' said Holly, 'to show to my mum and dad. Art is my mum's whole life.'

Phew! For a minute I thought Yasmin's mum was going to ring Joe and tell him his sculpture was still OK. Thank goodness none of Yasmin's uncles were in the house. They would certainly have fallen on it.

CHAPTER 13

My blood froze.
This smelt like trouble.

ALL AFTERNOON I FELT thrilled. It was great seeing people admire Joe's work. It was just too bad I couldn't tell him about it. When I got home I was just bursting to tell everybody about my wonderful day. Everybody had said Joe was a genius! But I knew I had to keep quiet. At least for a while. Joe would be furious if he knew I'd stolen – or even borrowed – his sculpture and lent it to Holly.

I was a bit on edge all evening in case Joe

noticed. Mum asked if I felt OK. I said I was just thinking.

'What about?' she asked.

I had to come up with something convincing, fast. 'Tree houses,' I said.

Mum sighed. 'I'm so sorry you can't have one, love. Maybe in the future we'll visit one somewhere.'

'It's OK,' I said. 'I've got one in my head. An imaginary one.'

'Good girl!' said Mum, and gave me a hug. I felt guilty, though. For once in my life I wasn't thinking about a tree house at all. I was wondering how long it would be before my crime was discovered. But the whole evening went by and Joe didn't say a thing.

Next day when I got to Yasmin's, there was a big van parked outside their house. It said 'Root and Branch – Tree Surgeon' on the side. There was a terrific roaring, ripping noise coming from Yasmin's back garden, and once I got inside the house it was even worse.

Yasmin and her mum welcomed me in sign language. We all covered our ears. Then the noise suddenly stopped.

'Sorry about that,' said Yasmin's mum. 'It *is* a

liddle bit noisy today. They're cutting down one of the trees at the back.'

'Oh no,' I said. I felt a bit sad. I always do when trees are cut down.

'This one has to go,' said Yasmin's mum. 'It's a liddle bit too near the house. Look . . .'

We went into the kitchen and looked out through the window. Yasmin's dad was out there with some men wearing hard hats. One of them had a chainsaw. The other was holding ropes.

'If we leave the tree, its roots might damage the foundations of the house,' said Yasmin's mum. 'The back wall could collapse.'

'Yeah,' said Yasmin. 'And the twigs scratch against my window at night. It's spooky. It gives me bad dreams.'

'We'll still have four trees anyway,' said Yasmin's mum. I felt really jealous. She looked at me.

'How are the plans for your liddle tree house coming along, Ruby?' she asked me. I told her I'd given up hope of having one. 'Oh dear, I'm so sorry,' she said. 'That seems such a shame.'

Just then Yasmin's dad came in from the garden and took his hard hat off. He smiled at me.

'Hello, Ruby!' he said. 'How's your family?'

'Very well, thank you, Mr Saffet,' I replied. Talking to Yasmin's dad is a bit like talking to the headmaster. Luckily, moments after I'd said hello, the front doorbell rang. 'Ah,' said Yasmin's dad. 'This will be Ron, I think.'

Ron is the man who does most of the fitted kitchens for Yasmin's dad. Ron looks a bit like Shrek. In fact, Yasmin and I secretly call him Shrek behind his back.

'Hi everybody!' said Ron as he came in through the kitchen door. He was grinning as usual.

'Come and have a look at this wood, Ron,' said Yasmin's dad. 'I was wondering if it might be possible to use some of it in the hand-built units.'

'Well, it'd have to be seasoned and treated first, of course,' said Ron. 'But let's have a look.'

They went out of the back door. The chainsaw started up again with a roar. Yasmin's house seemed very crowded and noisy today.

It was even more crowded at lunchtime. There was Holly and Zerrin, Mr and Mrs Saffet, the tree surgeon men and Ron all sitting and having a cup of tea. I felt a bit shy and I wished the men would go away and leave us in peace.

'Ruby!' said Holly quietly, on her way out afterwards. 'Could you possibly come home with me this afternoon? My mum wants to ask you about Joe's sculpture.'

'Yes, sure!' I said, surprised and a bit worried.

'You're going to wish you'd never stolen the damn thing!' whispered Holly.

My blood froze. This smelt like trouble. Maybe Holly's mum was going to be really cross about me stealing it.

'You're never going to be able to get away with it, now!' said Holly. 'We're in deep doo-doo, believe me!'

Terror gripped me. But despite Holly's frightening words, her eyes were dancing as if she was joking. Maybe Holly was a horrible person after all, and she'd set this trap just to get me into trouble!

'Ring your folks and tell them you'll be late,' said Holly, out loud this time. Suddenly she sounded calm and polite. 'Tell them you're coming home to tea with me and we'll bring you safe home – around seven or something.'

I nodded, but I was so scared I could hardly speak. I felt sick. My hands shook.

'Go on – ring them now,' said Holly, offering me her mobile. My head was whirling. Was Holly really nice and amazingly cool? Or was she as evil as her lipstick?

'Use the landline, Ruby!' said Yasmin's mum. I picked up the phone and dialled our number.

My heart was pounding away like mad. Apart from the trouble I was in with Holly's mum, I knew my mum would disapprove of me going to Holly's house. Even though she hadn't met Holly, she didn't like the sound of her. My mum can take against somebody for no reason at all.

Phew! It was the answering machine. Of course! Mum and Dad would be at work.

'Hello, this is me,' I said. 'I'm going to be late today, but I'm getting a lift home, so don't worry. I'll be back about seven.' I had managed not to mention Holly by name. I hoped Mum would think I was just staying late at Yasmin's.

'Brilliant!' said Holly. 'It's all fixed, then. See you later!' And she winked devilishly and went off back to work.

'Would you like to do some painting this afternoon?' asked Yasmin's mum. I nodded dumbly. I didn't care what I did. I was past caring.

Somehow all my paintings were of witches and daggers and sharks. And all the time I was painting, I was worrying about what Holly's mum would say.

My blood ran cold at the thought of it. I'd never met Mrs Helvellyn, but in my imagination she got bigger and bigger and more and more like an ogre, all afternoon. I couldn't tell Yasmin, because her mum was there all the time, making a cake and doing the crossword.

I was so scared of Holly's mum and the trouble I was in, that I would happily have flushed myself down the toilet if it meant I didn't have to go home with Holly. When Holly arrived back from work, she didn't even sit down for a cup of tea or anything.

'Ready, Ruby?' she asked. 'Mustn't be late for my mum, or she'll get in a strop.'

The thought of the massive ogre woman in a strop made my blood turn to ice. I had been planning to tell Holly how scared I was, but Zerrin came with us. She and Holly were busy all the time, arguing about something really random – something to do with the number of calories in a tub of hummus – so I just tagged along beside them in silent dread.

When we reached Holly's house, Zerrin waved goodbye. She was going off to her dance class.

'See you!' she said. 'Have a lovely tea!'

A lovely tea? Hardly likely. As Holly put her key in the door, I was almost fainting with terror.

CHAPTER 14

How completely
and totally brilliant!

THE DOOR SWUNG OPEN and we stepped inside Holly's house. I was amazed. It was like a museum or something. The hall had gold walls and was hung with strange eastern masks.

'Mum!' called Holly. 'We're back!' I followed, my heart beating fast. Now we were in a totally different room, a sort of kitchen-dining room. The walls were pale blue and absolutely covered in modern paintings: brilliant splashes

85

of jolly colour – red and pink and purple.

The floor was bare boards, and there was a big wooden table where a boy about Joe's age was sitting eating some nachos. He had thick blond hair and slightly gappy teeth, and he was plump.

'This is my evil brother Tom,' said Holly. 'Tom, this is Ruby. Joe Rogers' sister.'

Tom raised his clenched fist in a kind of salute.

'Respect,' he said.

'Tom wishes he was black,' said Holly. 'He's going to be a white rapper called The Ghostie. Where's Mum, Tom?'

'In the garden,' he said.

Just then Mrs Helvellyn came in, carrying a huge bunch of red flowers. She had the same thick fair hair as Tom but hers was cut in a bob. She had the same slightly gappy smile. And she was wearing a long straight black dress and a lot of chunky silver jewellery.

'Oh, Ruby!' she said. 'How nice! There are nachos – would you like some?'

'Yes, please,' I said. Holly laid a place for me. Tom was just finishing. There was a big bowl of salad on the table. I was hoping to avoid that as I could see olives in it.

'Your dad's teaching Joe to drive, yeah?' said Tom.

'Yes.'

'Lucky,' said Tom. 'My folks won't even get in a car with me. They suck.' Tom got up and strolled off, burping loudly.

'Tom!' called his mum in disgust.

'Scuse me, people,' said Tom, and vanished upstairs. Soon afterwards rap music could be heard. Teenage boys are so predictable.

'So, Ruby!' said Holly's mum. I'd got a pile of nachos on my plate and a glass of passion-fruit juice on the side, but I was still way too nervous to eat. 'I was truly amazed by Joe's sculpture. Tell me about it.'

'I was only borrowing it,' I said. 'I thought Holly might be interested.' My heart started to race. Although Holly's mum was obviously not an ogre, she still might disapprove of my stealing it and give me a hard time, and ring my mum.

'Yes, of course he can have it back,' said Holly's mum. 'But Holly's not the only one who's interested. I think he's very talented. Has he done any more like that?'

'Oh, loads,' I told her. 'His bedroom's full of them. Loads and loads.'

'Really?' Holly's mum smiled. Her lipstick was very pink, and some of it had got on to her teeth. It was quite funny, especially as she was so elegant otherwise. 'You see, Ruby,' she went on, 'I don't know whether Holly's told you, but I've got a little art gallery in the High Street. It's called Jazz. Maybe you've seen it?'

My mind went blank. I couldn't remember a gallery. It seemed rude to say so, though.

'I'm not sure . . .' I said.

'Anyway, I have exhibitions there all the time,' said Holly's mum. 'And I was wondering if maybe we could do an exhibition for Joe. The thing is . . .' She hesitated and looked a bit embarrassed. 'I've got a gap in my schedule for the week after next.

Somebody's cancelled.' She looked at me hopefully. I just went on chomping my nachos. I was hoping she'd remember that I was a young girl, not a jet-setting artist's agent. (Although give me time . . .)

'What I was hoping,' Holly's mum went on, 'was that I might be able to come round and see Joe's work, and talk to him, and see if he likes the idea of an exhibition. Would you mind asking him? And it's all a bit of a rush, I'm afraid, because of the cancellation.'

'I'll tell him as soon as I get home,' I said. It would be an amazing break for Joe. But I'd have to confess to stealing his model in the first place.

'Thank you, Ruby! I hope your parents won't think it's pushy of me or anything.'

'Oh no!' I said. 'I'm sure they'll be pleased.'

I was worried, though. Mum didn't like the sound of Holly, and she'd got this stupid prejudice about piercings. Maybe she wouldn't want to have anything to do with Mrs Helvellyn either. Maybe she'd be a bit frosty about having her over, even to see Joe's stuff.

After we'd finished eating, Holly asked if I'd like to go up and see her room. I did. It was amazing! The walls were actually black and there were huge heaps of jewellery and witches' hats and eyeballs that glowed in the dark. She had a laptop up there and she played me a bit of her DVD of *The Rocky Horror Picture Show*. Then it was time to go home.

Holly's mum drove me home, and we went through the centre of town. As we were going down the High Street, she slowed down and pointed to a shop with mirrors and spotlights, and bronze statues of bulls and deer in the window.

'That's the gallery,' she said. I gasped. It was amazing – so cool! Imagine Joe's stuff being displayed there! How completely and totally brilliant!

Mrs Helvellyn dropped me off at my door and then drove away. She said she didn't want to 'intrude'. So it was up to me to explain the whole thing. I was, of course, more terrified than *ever*.

I tried hard to get myself into a gangsterish mood, to give myself courage. But it didn't work. For a start, I'd have to 'fess up to stealing the sculpture. Joe would be furious that I'd even been in his room. And even though it was so obviously a big break for him, he might not buy it.

What if he got into one of his sulky moods, and refused to show Holly's mum his work or anything? As I walked up the front path, half of me was fizzing with hope, and the other half was sick with fear.

CHAPTER 15
Wait! Stop! Don't go!

MUM WAS ASLEEP with her mouth open, Dad was behind the paper, and Joe was texting somebody. Meanwhile, on the TV, some people were fighting in a pub, in a vain attempt to attract my family's attention.

'Hi, guys!' I said, and sat down on the rug by the coffee table. Dad gave me a smile. I just had to tell them this evening. Mrs Helvellyn might ring up tomorrow wanting to talk about it. Holy Baloney! She might just ring up *tonight*!

I glanced secretly at Joe. He was frowning at his

mobile, but kind of smiling to himself. How angry would he be when he knew I'd stolen his model and shown it to people? He might do something terrible to all three of my monkeys.

Soon the TV programme ended, and Dad jabbed the remote to switch it off. He sighed.

'What a load of old codswallop,' he said. 'I'm going to give up watching soaps. I'm going to give up watching football too.'

'Hey, Dad!' said Joe. 'No need to go that far. Man Gives Up Watching Football. Insanity Suspected.'

Mum stirred in her sleep.

'*Well, what time's the next train?*' she said in a weird zombie-type dreaming voice. '*I've got to get to London. I know they have toilets there.*' Then she suddenly woke up. 'Oh my goodness!' she said. 'I was asleep! I'm so sorry! Did I snore?'

This had to be the moment when I told them. They were at least all awake now, and the TV was off. My heart went into thudding overdrive.

'I've got something to tell you,' I started, speaking in a hectic rush. Joe got up from his chair and slouched towards the door.

'Wait! Stop! Don't go, Joe! It's all about you!' I yelled. Joe stopped and scowled.

'Wha?' he grunted.

I told them that I'd gone home to have tea at Holly's and that I'd just got talking about Joe's sculptures and Mrs Helvellyn had got very interested. I talked really fast so Mum couldn't get a word in. I saw her frown when I mentioned the dreaded word 'Holly'.

I decided not to mention anything about stealing the model from Joe's wardrobe. I knew I'd have to mention it before tomorrow, because Holly's mum would let the cat out of the bag, but right now I thought I'd stick to the good news.

'And the good news is, she's got a free week at the gallery the week after next, and if she likes Joe's stuff, he could have an exhibition there in that week,' I said. 'So she wants to come tomorrow to see all his model thingies. Sculptures.'

'She's not coming up to my room,' said Joe with one of his darkest scowls. Honestly, some people!

'We could set all your models out in the garden!' said Mum. 'The weather forecast's good for the next few days.'

'I'll mow the lawn!' said Dad.

'We can give them tea and sandwiches out there!' said Mum. 'We can make some of those chocolate brownies!'

'They're not supposed to be sculptures,' said Joe sulkily. 'They're models for installations. They shouldn't really be small like that. They're supposed to be big – big enough to fill a room. Or even a whole street.'

'Oh shut up, Joe, you idiot!' said Mum, getting up excitedly and clearing away the tea tray. 'You never know what it might lead to. Somebody posh might come in and see your models, and offer you the chance to do a big one in public.'

I couldn't help laughing then, and even Joe kind of sniggered a bit. Mum looked puzzled.

'What have I said now, you disgusting crea-tures?' she asked. Then she shook her head, laughed, and carried the tray out. Joe was still smiling. This was my moment.

'I borrowed one of your models a couple of days ago,' I said. 'To show her. Well, to show Holly actually.' Joe looked shocked. And maybe it was my imagination, but it seemed for a second as if he blushed slightly.

'Which one?' he asked.

'The one like a duck's skeleton with the egg inside and the egg is an eye really. It was in your wardrobe.'

'Never go in my wardrobe again or you're dead meat,' said Joe. 'And anyway, that one's rubbish. You should have taken the Eiffel Tower dressed up in a fur coat.'

But I could tell he wasn't really cross. Phew!

CHAPTER 16

Fantastic! Fabulous!

N EXT DAY, EVERYTHING was ready.
The lawn had never been so mowed. It
looked as if it had been to the hairdresser's. At
one end, under a big sun umbrella, was a table
with tea things set out. The whole house smelt of
chocolate brownies. And all Joe's model things
were set out on the low wall that separates the
lawn from the vegetable garden.

We were all in the kitchen when the doorbell
rang. Mum was giving the teaspoons an extra
polish.

'Go and answer the door, Ruby!' she whispered. 'They're your guests.'

My heart was thudding away like mad as I ran to open the door. And there stood Mrs Helvellyn, Holly and even Tom.

Mrs Helvellyn was looking totally fabulous in a cream dress and blue glass earrings. You could tell she'd just washed her hair and her lipstick was a lovely shade of bubble-gum pink. Holly was wearing her usual bright red lipstick, but she wasn't all in black. She had on a nice pale green blouse, and she was carrying her camera. Tom was just ordinary in a baseball cap. I hoped Mum wouldn't be put off by Holly's piercings.

'Come in!' I said. Mrs Helvellyn swooped down and kissed me on both cheeks. She smelt nice. But I hoped she wasn't going to kiss everybody. Especially Joe. Holly kissed me too.

'Hope my mum isn't too embarrassing!' she whispered.

'Hope *mine* isn't!' I whispered back. The mums had already met, and Mrs Helvellyn was being invited out to the garden, where Joe was waiting, looking as if he'd like to murder everyone. But I knew he was excited really.

Right away, Mrs Helvellyn started swooning

over Joe's sculptures. Tom and Dad got talking about cars or something. Thank God I'm not a boy. I couldn't talk about cars for a split second.

Holly started taking photos. Most of the photos were of Joe's work, but I noticed she did take a few ones of Joe when he wasn't looking. Then she came up to me.

'Smile please, Ruby!' she said. 'I want a portrait of The Artist's Sister. Say cheese!'

'Boursin,' I said, trying to be clever.

'You prune!' said Holly. 'That one will look like you're burping.' She took a few more.

'Stop it,' I said. 'I haven't ironed my hair today.'

Holly laughed and sat with me on the grass. I noticed Joe was looking at us as he stood obediently by Holly's mum, soaking up her raptures. Mrs Helvellyn was in art heaven.

'Oh my God! Fantastic! Fabulous! . . . And look at this one! . . . Oh, and here's Big Ben dressed as a witch! How witty! . . . Oh, and look at this boat with wings!'

'My mum has fallen for Joe's work,' whispered Holly. 'She'll never leave him alone now. He has acquired a middle-aged female stalker. Every teenage boy should have one. The ultimate fashion accessory.'

I got the giggles. Holly looked around, sighed in a happy kind of way and put her arm round me.

'I *love* your garden!' she said. I was amazed.

'The trouble with our garden,' I said, 'is that we haven't got a big tree.' Holly looked sympathetic.

'Oh, your wonderful tree house idea.' She looked around. 'I see the problem.'

'I couldn't have one here,' I said. 'I was hoping to have one out in the country somewhere, but I've given up on that now, because . . . Well, I couldn't raise the money.'

'But it would be a bit of a nuisance anyway,

always having to go out to the country whenever you wanted to be in your tree house,' said Holly. 'Never mind, though, Rube.' She gave me a squeeze. 'I've had to give up on my iguana.'

'Oh!' I said, disappointed. 'Why?'

'I realised that the best place for an iguana is the rainforest or wherever it is they live,' she said. 'But I'm planning a trip to see them in the wild, and you can come. In fact, we'll go and live in the rainforest.'

'In a tree house!' I said.

'Exactly!' said Holly. 'With iguanas and monkeys wall-to-wall! Except there won't be any walls!'

She squeezed me again, so hard that I sort of barked, like an unattractive small dog. I so adored her. I'm going to be exactly like Holly when I'm a teenager.

'Well, Joe,' said Mrs Helvellyn when she'd examined every one of Joe's models in detail, 'I'm terribly, terribly impressed. I'd love to stage an exhibition of your sculptures the week after next. What do you think?'

Joe went bright red and did one of his special pleased frowns. I hope she realised it wasn't just an ordinary rude frown.

'Whatever,' he said. 'Yeah, cool.' I suppose that

was quite polite, by his standards. At this point Mum saved the day by bringing out the tea.

After Holly's family had gone, we all carried Joe's sculptures back up to his room. Mum and Dad went downstairs to the kitchen but I hung around for a minute, looking at the bird-boat model which I'd destroyed.

'I'm sorry I trashed that model of yours,' I said. 'But you shouldn't make me lose my temper.'

'Local Girl Loses Temper,' said Joe. 'Bus Flattened and Primary School Hurled into the Air.'

'I did make it up to you in a way, though,' I said. 'By setting up your exhibition thingy.'

'Well, don't expect any thanks,' said Joe. 'Although if you're really lucky, to show my appreciation, I might kick you downstairs.' By our standards this amounted to a declaration of brotherly love.

Life was getting better. Joe was talking to me now instead of sulking and glaring. It always makes things a bit easier if the male animals aren't in a grim old strop about something.

I went to my bedroom and lay down on the bed with my monkeys. It was only a few days now to my birthday, but I knew that my dream of a tree house had gone for ever. Unless Holly had really meant it about going to live in the rainforest.

I felt a bit sad about the tree house. But as long as Joe's exhibition was a success, and Holly was still nice to me, life would be much more birth-dayish anyway.

CHAPTER 17
It's a mystery!

A FEW DAYS LATER the birthday actually arrived. It was on a Saturday, which was great as it meant that Mum wouldn't have to be at work. I woke up early because I was so excited, even though I knew there wouldn't be much of a fuss. I got dressed quickly and ran downstairs.

Mum and Dad were sitting having breakfast, but they sang 'Happy Birthday' even though their mouths were full of toast. Typical! So unstylish. Still, I was pleased, and I hugged and kissed them both.

There were some cards and presents from aunts and uncles, and Granny and Grandpa, and Nanny and Gramps. But I couldn't help noticing that there was nothing from Mum and Dad. Or Joe (who, by the way, was still in bed – of course.)

But I didn't mention it in case Mum and Dad just hadn't been able to afford anything. They're always going on about how hard up they are. So I just sat down and tried to decide which cereal to have.

'Well?' said Mum.

I looked around. The room looked normal. Mum looked normal. Dad looked normal. There was no cute puppy with a bow tied round its neck.

'Well what?' I asked.

'Aren't you wondering what we're going to give you, petal?' asked Mum.

'Well,' I said shyly, 'I thought we might not be able to afford anything, and that's all right . . . It's fine.'

'Aah, bless her!' said Mum to Dad. 'No, don't be daft, petal. Of course we're going to give you something. After breakfast you and I are going to get in the car and go and collect Yasmin . . . and then you're going to have a Mystery Day Out.'

'A Mystery Day Out?' I said. My heart gave a funny little jump. 'Brilliant! Where are we going?'

'It's a mystery,' said Mum with a wink. I gobbled up my cereal. I could hardly wait.

It was a shame, but Dad and Joe couldn't come. Joe would be very busy all day because his exhibition opened soon, so he had to be at the gallery helping Mrs Helvellyn to arrange the models. And Dad was going to help him. I knew Joe's exhibition was mega-important, but I wished they could have come on the Mystery Day Out with us instead.

'Are we going to the sea?' I asked. We live miles from the sea. We only usually go there when we're staying with Auntie Megan in North Wales.

'No, it's not the sea, love,' said Mum. 'It's too far to drive all the way to the sea. But in a way it's better than the seaside – I promise, you'll have loads of thrills!'

A thrill ran through me immediately, just thinking about the thrills. We got in the car and waved goodbye to Dad. (Joe was still in bed.)

First we called at Yasmin's. She was waiting with a present, wrapped in wonderful paper covered with blue stars and yellow comets. I unwrapped it right away.

It was a fabulous gangster outfit! Pinstripe suit, black shirt, wide tie and a trilby hat. 'Oh my gawd!' I screamed. 'I want to wear it NOW!' So I got changed while Mum was driving down the road. (Nobody saw.)

'How did you get it?' I asked Yasmin.

'My mum ordered it on the internet,' said Yasmin. 'It arrived last week. It was a big secret and I nearly told you twice.'

'I love it!' I said.

Yasmin had brought her Game Boy. We played on it constantly – and Mum didn't even ask us to turn the sound down. We drove out of town and along the motorway for ages and ages. Then, suddenly we arrived at the gates of The Mystery Place.

CHAPTER 18

I almost exploded with rage

IT WAS A SAFARI PARK! I'd never been to one, but I'd always wanted to. We drove slowly along winding little roads. There were huge shady trees with actual *lions* lying down on the grass under them. It was so amazing to see them right up close like that.

But best of all were the monkeys! They were everywhere. The car slowed right down so it was hardly moving, and they jumped up on the front and played with the windscreen wipers. One of them rubbed his bottom against the glass. Gross!

We screamed with laughter.

There was a tiny baby monkey, clinging to its mother's fur. I wanted to stay for ever. In fact, I was quite tempted to jump out of the car and run away and live with them.

Once we'd been through the park, there was the best adventure playground I'd ever seen, with a huge tree in the middle. And guess what! There was a tree house built in it, with rope bridges and everything. It was massive, and we spent ages climbing about in it.

'So you see?' said Yasmin. 'You got your tree house after all!' I grinned. Obviously, I would rather have had my own tree house rather than having to share one with loads of other kids I'd never met before, but I didn't want to sound ungrateful.

After that we had a pizza in the open-air café, and then we went home. Yasmin and I were so tired, we slept all the way back in the car. We woke up when the car stopped and the engine was switched off.

'Wakey, wakey, girls!' said Mum. 'We're home!'

We yawned and stretched and blinked. It was still light, of course. Having my birthday in the summer holidays is really cool. It never falls on a school day. Yasmin's is in January – I feel really sorry for her.

We piled out of the car and went indoors. Dad and Joe were having a cup of tea and looking a bit tired and dusty.

'Once we'd fixed up the exhibition, we came home and cleared out the shed,' said Dad.

'Yeah,' added Joe sarcastically. 'More fun than I've had for ages.'

We told them all about our day. Mum got some juice for us and produced a little birthday cake which had been hidden in the back of the fridge. Everybody sang 'Happy Birthday' again and I blew the candles out.

'Has it been a good birthday, then, love?' asked Mum.

'Oh yes, thanks!' I said. 'The best ever!' I hugged and kissed Mum, Dad and Yasmin, and to show my sisterly affection, I bit Joe on the ankle.

'OK, then,' said Mum. 'If you've finished your juice, just nip up and tidy your room, and then we'll take Yasmin home.'

'Tidy my room?' I almost exploded with rage. 'What!? Tidy my room on my birthday? Oh please, NO!'

'Come on, Ruby love,' said Mum. 'You promised

to tidy it every day, remember? Every day after supper. It'll only take five minutes.'

Dad and Joe were looking at me and grinning. How could they be so mean on my birthday?

'I'll do it tomorrow!' I pleaded. I *so* didn't want to do it. I so didn't want Yasmin to see my mess. 'It's not fair on Yasmin!' I said. 'I'll tidy up tonight at bedtime.'

I really couldn't believe my mum could be so harsh.

'Now don't spoil your lovely day by being a stubborn little so-and-so,' said Mum. 'Just go and do as I say, please.'

'I'll help,' said Yasmin. 'Come on, Ruby. It won't take a minute.'

I got down from the table in a massive sulk. I couldn't believe my mum had forced me into this on my birthday, of all days. I stomped up the stairs. Welcome back to the real world, sucker.

CHAPTER 19
I don't believe it!

I SHOVED MY BEDROOM door open ...
And SCREAMED ALOUD! Several times!
Guess what! There was a *tree house* in there! A
TREE HOUSE in my bedroom!

'Oh my gawd!' I screeched. 'Oh no! I don't believe
it! Oh my gawd! It's *amaaaaaaaaaaaazing!*'

There were huge branches stretching right up
from the floor to the ceiling. And there was a
little wooden hut sitting on a platform nestled in
among the branches. The platform was about as
high as my head. There was a rope ladder you

had to climb to get up into the house itself.

'Go on!' said Yasmin. 'Climb up and have a look!'

My family was coming upstairs, laughing. They had staged the biggest surprise. When I had said this had been the best birthday ever, I'd had no idea *this* was waiting for me.

I climbed up the rope ladder and crawled into the tree house. There was a mattress in there, all made up as a bed, and the monkeys were in there, looking rather surprised.

Yasmin climbed up too, clumsily as usual. She nearly fell off. Then we sat down inside the tree house together. It even had a kind of thatched roof. There were a couple of windows to look out of, and you could close the door with a sort of canvas flap.

Somebody had painted the walls and ceiling of the room a bright sky-blue, so it was just like being outdoors.

'Do you like it?' asked Mum.

'Like it!?' I shouted. 'I absolutely ADORE it!'

'Dad and Joe made it,' said Mum, 'while I took you to the safari park, out of the way.'

'Ron the carpenter helped,' said Dad. 'You know, Yasmin's dad's chappie.'

'Shrek built it!' said Yasmin with a grin. So Yasmin had been in on the secret all the time and she'd never said a word! How completely amazing.

'The branches came from Yasmin's garden,' said Dad.

'That tree that was cut down,' said Yasmin.

'And Joe designed it,' said Mum.

'It's an installation,' said Joe.

'It was all Joe's idea!' said Mum. 'It's a work of art, petal!'

'Holly helped,' said Joe. 'She painted the walls and the ceiling.'

I peeped out of the doorway down at Joe. He was grinning all over his face.

'Thanks, Joe,' I went on. 'Remind me to bite you more gently in future.'

'And the great advantage of having your tree house indoors,' said Mum, 'is that you can still enjoy it all through the winter.'

I knew she was right. My only problem was going to be tearing myself away from it. I just might spend the *rest of my life* right here.

CHAPTER 20
Clear off or
I'll set the dogs on you

JOE'S EXHIBITION OPENED a couple of days later. There was a sort of party to launch it. Some photographers came and a reporter from the local paper. Mrs Helvellyn had put prices on all his models – from fifty pounds to over a hundred pounds! I couldn't believe it.

Holly was acting as a waitress, handing round canapes and champagne. She was wearing a tuxedo and a bow tie and she looked sublime.

'Have a canape, Rogers,' she said to Joe. I liked the way she called him 'Rogers'.

'Too nervous to eat,' said Joe, waving the canapes away. 'Local Artist Pukes Over Own Sculptures. Claims It Was Conceptual Art Event. Celebs Disgusted.'

'You're the celeb, you idiot,' said Holly. 'You know: *It's my party and I'll puke if I want to.*' Then somebody came for a canape and she disappeared into a different conversation.

Mrs Helvellyn looked rich and powerful in a shimmering sky-blue dress and huge pearl earrings. Mum and Dad were slightly scruffy by comparison. Mum had a new dress, but it was a bit tight across her fat little bum. However, although I felt slightly ashamed of my family's lack of style, somehow it only made me love them more.

And anyway, Uncle Tristram came all the way from Bath. Amazingly, he had managed to acquire a tall Dutch girlfriend called Astrid with wild Afro hair, tawny skin and gold lipstick. So at least there was one person from our family who was obviously not a nerd.

There was a real buzz and I overheard a lot of people saying things like: 'Amazing!', 'Original!', 'So talented!' I stood next to Joe and pulled a Joe sort of face so everyone would know I was his sister.

Yasmin came with all her family. In fact, Mr Saffet was the first person to buy one of the sculptures.

'I'll have that one that looks like an aeroplane,' he said, getting out his cheque book.

'Dad!' hissed Yasmin. 'It's not an aeroplane, it's a hawk!'

After she'd finished handing round the food

and drink, Holly got her camera and took loads more photos. It was a great day. The best.

I mean, the day when I'd got my birthday tree house was the *very* best day, obviously. But this was wonderful in a completely different way. Because it wasn't about me, it was about Joe. And though I frequently want to drop horrible things on his head, I also want him to be a mega-success, a total star.

Two or three days later it was Mum and Dad's wedding anniversary. They went out for a special romantic dinner at a restaurant called Gino's. Joe and I stayed at home and watched a movie about zombies. I was behind the sofa with my eyes closed most of the time, although the zombies were really funny.

Suddenly there was a knock on the door. I froze.

'It's clearly a zombie,' said Joe. 'You go.'

'You go!' I said. 'You're supposed to be the babysitter.'

'OK, I'll go if you come too,' said Joe. 'Home Alone: Local Youngsters Eaten by Zombies While Their Heartless Parents Party at Gino's.'

'Come on, you wuss,' I said. 'It's not even dark.'

We opened the door and there stood Holly. She

was carrying a big leather bag and looking divine. However, she wasn't as Gothic as usual. Just as I'd started saving up for my first red lipstick, she'd stopped wearing red. She hadn't got any rings in her piercings either, just a few tiny sparkly stones. Her hair wasn't scraped up or anything, it was just hanging down quietly minding its own business. She was wearing a green dress and green shoes. She looked so fabulous, I was surprised Joe didn't faint right there on the doormat. If he wasn't going to fall for her, I'd just have to do the decent thing and found a fan club for her myself. I'd already decided that when I grew up, my gang would be called 'The Hellcats' in her honour.

'Good evening!' said Holly with a pouty smile. 'I'm looking for a Mr J. Rogers and his devoted sister Ruby.'

'Never heard of them,' said Joe. 'Clear off or I'll set the dogs on you.'

'Come in, Holly!' I said. 'Would you like a Coke and some Doritos?'

'Thank goodness somebody's got some manners here!' said Holly, tripping lightly over the threshold.

'You smell nice,' I said.

'It's Calvin Klein,' said Holly. 'And thanks, I will

have some Doritos, though not Coke. It rots your teeth.'

'Joe could make you a cappucino,' I said. 'We've got a machine.'

We all went into the kitchen. I wasn't quite sure what to do. Holly's eyes looked kind of sparkly, and I wondered if she had really come to see Joe, and whether I should make an excuse and go off to my tree house upstairs. But although I adored my tree house more than anything else in the world, I wanted to stay with Holly.

Besides, Joe seemed even more useless than usual when she was around. Even now he was fumbling with the coffee beans and spilling some on the floor. Ultimately, though, he got it organised, and we went and sat down in the lounge.

'OK,' said Holly. 'Do you want the good news or the bad news?'

'The bad news,' said Joe. 'Don't bother with good news, it's always such a cliché.'

'What's a cliché?' I asked.

'Something very dull that everybody does,' said Holly.

'Well, I want the good news, even if he doesn't,' I said.

'Well,' said Holly, 'the bad news is that you're

going to have to part with five of your beloved sculptures, Joe, because Mum's sold them. Five! And we're only halfway through the week.' She reached inside her leather bag.

'Here's a cheque for three hundred and twenty smackeroonies.' She handed it over with a glamorous grin. Joe looked at the cheque and went bright red.

'You are now officially the richest boy in the area and will be pursued by hordes of bimbos,' said Holly. 'I, of course, prefer monkeys. Speaking of which – I've got something for you, Ruby.'

She handed over a parcel wrapped in starry blue paper. I ripped it open. It was a fabulous big book about monkeys.

'My favourites are those Japanese monkeys who bathe in the hot springs while it's snowing all around them,' said Holly. 'I'm not sure about the ones with bright red bottoms. I think they should be forced to wear cycling shorts.'

'Oh, thanks so much, Holly!' I said, flicking over the pages and drooling over the wonderful photos of monkeys having fun – mostly in the rainforest.

'Well, I didn't give you a proper birthday present,' said Holly. 'And we mustn't have you getting jealous of Joe with his great wealth.'

'We can't all be art millionaires,' I said. 'I expect Joe's told you – he thinks I'm a waste of space.'

'What?!' cried Holly, and she turned on Joe, showing her teeth like a tiger. 'After all Ruby's done to promote your career? Joe Rogers, you are a total dork!'

'I didn't mean it unkindly,' said Joe, squirming slightly on the sofa. 'When I described her as a waste of space, I meant it in the nicest possible way.'

'Oh, that's all right, then,' I said and whacked his

knee with a teaspoon. He ignored me, but in the nicest possible way. It seemed our relationship was improving.

There was a strange little pause. Holly fiddled with her hair. Joe fiddled with his trainers.

'So . . . what are your plans for the summer, maestro?' asked Holly.

'My parents were giving me a hard time about getting a job,' said Joe with a sly grin. 'But I won't have to now.' He waved his cheque.

'Oh, right,' said Holly. She looked really disappointed for a moment. 'Because they're recruiting new staff at the place where Zerrin and I work. I said I'd ask you if you were available. I know it's mind-numbing torture, but it pays well and we have the best time.'

'Er . . .' said Joe, looking doubtful. *Go for it, go for it, you idiot!* I thought. It was *so obvious* that Holly was mad about him, and wanted an excuse to see more of him, and here he was mumbling and frowning as if she'd asked him to eat concrete in the pouring rain. 'I dunno . . .' he said. 'I'm so lazy. Doesn't really sound like my thing.'

'Oh, come *on!*' said Holly. 'Don't tell me you're too grand to pack airline lunches!' Joe shrugged.

'Maybe . . .' he stalled. 'Maybe that's just what I

am,' he said. 'Local Artist Allergic to Honest Work. Getting Up Early Ruins the Creative Process.'

'Well, stuff it. Don't then,' said Holly. Just for a split second, she looked really cross and embarrassed. I wondered if Joe was only saying no because I was there. Maybe I should go up to my tree house right now. I got up.

'Where are you going?' said Holly. 'Sit down, Ruby. You mustn't miss this. Since his Lordship is in the mood for newspaper headlines, get a load of this one.' And she pulled a newspaper from her bag and threw it across to him.

There he was, on the front page! There was a photo of him standing next to Holly's mum and holding one of his sculptures.

The headline was: 'Local Art Student Wins Praise from London Critics.' It said that famous arty people from London had visited the show and said Joe was the new Leonardo da Vinci – well, more or less.

Joe was speechless for a moment. He went a bit pink. His blushing mechanism was certainly working overtime. I grinned at Holly and pulled a face which meant: my brother, though described as the new da Vinci, is in some respects the lowest form of life.

Holly gave me a smile and did something cute with her eyebrows which showed she agreed totally.

'OK, then, Ruby,' she said. 'Take me up to that tree house of yours. I've had enough hassle for one day.'

I took her up to my tree house. Joe stayed downstairs. I heard him switch on the DVD again. He's such a plonker. Holly and I sat up in my tree house, sharing the Doritos and making monkey noises. Downstairs, there was the occa-

sional screech and horrid murderous gurgle as Joe festered with his TV zombies.

It was quite clear what my next secret plan was going to have to be: getting my idiot brother off that sofa and into the arms of the divine Miss Hell. Still, it was exactly the kind of work that appealed to me. So I was determined to have it all sorted by . . . oh, I don't know. Maybe the middle of next week?